Y0-BYA-612

jB Y87b
Bock, Hal.
Steve Young

**DO NOT REMOVE
CARDS FROM POCKET**

MAY 0 3 1997

**ALLEN COUNTY PUBLIC LIBRARY
FORT WAYNE, INDIANA 46802**

You may return this book to any agency, branch,
or bookmobile of the Allen County Public Library.

DEMCO

FOOTBALL LEGENDS

Troy Aikman

Terry Bradshaw

Jim Brown

Dan Marino

Joe Montana

Joe Namath

Walter Payton

Jerry Rice

Barry Sanders

Deion Sanders

Emmitt Smith

Steve Young

CHELSEA HOUSE PUBLISHERS

STEVE YOUNG

Hal Bock

Introduction by
Chuck Noll

CHELSEA HOUSE PUBLISHERS
New York · Philadelphia

Allen County Public Library
900 Webster Street
PO Box 2270
Fort Wayne, IN 46801-2270

Produced by Daniel Bial and Associates
New York, New York

Picture research by Alan Gottlieb
Cover illustration by Bill Vann

Copyright © 1996 Chelsea House Publishers, a division of Main Line
Book Co. All rights reserved. Printed and bound in the United States
of America.

3 5 7 9 8 6 4 2

Bock, Hal.
    Steve Young / by Hal Bock.
    p. cm. — (Football legends)
    Includes bibliographical references and index.
    Summary: A biography of the talented quarterback who led the
San Francisco Giants to victory in the 1995 Super Bowl.
    ISBN 0-7910-2499-7
    1. Young, Steve, 1961- —Juvenile literature. 2. Football
players—United States—Biography—Juvenile literature. 3
San Francisco 49ers (Football team)—Juvenile literature.
[1. Young, Steve, 1961- . 2. Football players.] I. Title.
II. Series.
GV939. Y69B63 1996   95-182227
96. 332'092—dc20   CIP
[B]   AC

CONTENTS

A WINNING ATTITUDE

Chuck Noll

Don't ever fall into the trap of believing, "I could never do that. And I won't even try—I don't want to embarrass myself." After all, most top athletes had no idea what they could accomplish when they were young. A secret to the success of every star quarterback and sure-handed receiver is that they tried. If they had not tried, if they had not persevered, they would never have discovered how far they could go and how much they could achieve.

You can learn about trying hard and overcoming challenges by being a sports fan. Or you can take part in organized sports at any level, in any capacity. The student messenger at my high school is now president of a university. A reserve ballplayer who got very little playing time in high school now owns a very successful business. Both of them benefited by the lesson of perseverance that sports offers. The main point is that you don't have to be a Hall of Fame athlete to reap the benefits of participating in sports.

In math class, I learned that the whole is equal to the sum of its parts. But that is not always the case when you are dealing with people. Sports has taught me that the whole is either greater than or less than the sum of its parts, depending on how well the parts work together. And how the parts work together depends on how they really understand the concept of teamwork.

Most people believe that teamwork is a fifty-fifty proposition. But true teamwork is seldom, if ever, fifty-fifty. Teamwork is *whatever it takes to get the job done*. There is no time for the measurement of contributions, no time for anything but concentrating on your job.

One year, my Pittsburgh Steelers were playing the Houston Oilers in the Astrodome late in the season, with the division championship on the line. Our offensive line was hard hit by the flu, our starting quarterback was out with an injury, and we were having difficulty making a first down. There was tremendous pressure on our defense to perform well—and they rose to the occasion. If the players on the defensive unit had been measuring their contribution against the offense's contribution, they would have given up and gone home. Instead, with a "whatever it takes" attitude, they increased their level of concentration and performance, forced turnovers, and got the ball into field goal range for our offense. Thanks to our defense's winning attitude, we came away with a victory.

Believing in doing whatever it takes to get the job done is what separates a successful person from someone who is not as successful. Nobody can give you this winning outlook; you have to develop it. And I know from experience that it can be learned and developed on the playing field.

My favorite people on the football field have always been offensive linemen and defensive backs. I say this because it takes special people to perform well in jobs in which there is little public recognition when they are doing things right but are thrust into the spotlight as soon as they make a mistake. That is exactly what happens to a lineman whose man sacks the quarterback or a defensive back who lets his receiver catch a touchdown pass. They know the importance of being part of a group that believes in teamwork and does not point fingers at one another.

Sports can be a learning situation as much as it can be fun. And that's why I say, "Get involved. Participate."

CHUCK NOLL, the Pittsburgh Steelers head coach from 1969–1991, led his team to four Super Bowl victories—the most by any coach. Widely respected as an innovator on both offense and defense, Noll was inducted into the Pro Football Hall of Fame in 1993.

1

SWEET REDEMPTION

As Steve Young brought the San Francisco 49ers to the line of scrimmage, he was feeling pretty good. The first two plays of the Super Bowl had gone smoothly—a four-yard pitch to fullback William Floyd and then 11 yards and a first down to wide receiver John Taylor.

The pregame jitters, so natural in the Super Bowl, were beginning to settle down. Young already had his team at the San Diego 44. Now he called signals for the third offensive play of the game, a pass to Jerry Rice. As he looked over the defense, he saw something he had not seen in the films. Bill Arnsparger, the defensive guru of the Chargers, gave Young a new look, pulling the linebackers up tighter. Young had picked San Diego apart with short passes in their first meeting earlier in the season and Arnsparger decided that that would not happen again.

Steve Young celebrates after throwing a touchdown pass to Jerry Rice on the third play of Super Bowl XXIX. Young did not know it at the time, but this set a record for fastest score in Super Bowl history.

This could be a problem. For an instant, Young considered changing the play at the line, maybe calling an audible. Joe Montana might have done that and everything Young had ever done with the 49ers was measured against Montana, who had taken San Francisco to four Super Bowl championships.

But Montana was not around any more. This was Steve Young's time and Steve Young's team. There would be no second-guessing. Young had All-Pro Jerry Rice going against a spotty San Diego secondary. He would take his chances and stay with the original play, one of the first 15 the 49ers had scripted before the game in a carefully planned attack.

Young took the snap from center Bart Oates and threw for Rice slanting over the middle. The wide receiver sliced between San Diego's safeties and sprinted for the end zone. It was a 44-yard touchdown—the quickest strike in Super Bowl history. After three offensive plays and 1 minute, 24 seconds of playing time, San Francisco had a 7–0 lead.

"I knew Arnsparger would come up with some wrinkles," Young said later. "They threw a new defense at Jerry on the first touchdown. It had to be a dagger in their hearts that Jerry ran right through a defense he had never seen before for a touchdown."

Before this day was over, Young would twist that dagger five more times.

San Diego, set back on its heels by the quick strike, had no immediate answer. The Chargers went three plays and out and once more Young led the 49ers' offense on the field. This is an offense that does not play football by the old rules. "Most offenses take what the defense gives them," San Francisco linebacker Gary Plummer said. "Ours takes what it wants."

And right then, it wanted more points.

After three plays, the Niners were at midfield again, positioned there in part on a 21-yard scramble by Young, whose running abilities add an extra dimension to the San Francisco at tack. Now he dropped back to pass again. Running back Ricky Watters grabbed the perfectly thrown ball in full stride, broke a couple of tackles in the leaky secondary, and loped into the end zone on a 51-yard touchdown (TD) play.

After seven offensive plays, San Francisco led 14–0.

Before the first half was over, Young would throw a five-yard TD pass to Floyd and a second one to Watters, this time for six yards. By halftime, he had completed 17 of 23 attempts for 239 yards, four TDs, and no interceptions. San Francisco led 28–10 and it seemed like the sky was the limit. In fact, though, Young was a little angry with himself. He had misfired on a pass to tight end Brent Jones. "I missed him and I was upset because it could have put the game away earlier," Young said.

It was not said in a bragging way. That is not Steve Young's style. He is the most down-to-earth, Super Bowl most valuable player (MVP) you can imagine. He was just stating facts. And the fact is this 49ers offense is so efficient that the quarterback gets annoyed with himself when he messes it up.

And that is not very often.

By game's end, Young had a Super Bowl record of six TD passes—more in one game than Terry Bradshaw, Roger Staubach, or even a guy named Montana. He totaled 325 yards on 24 for

36 passing, and in his spare time, he also ran five times for 49 yards as the game's leading rusher in a 49–26 rout. It was a brilliant performance and when it was over, he tried to figure out what to do with the MVP award, a car that is far too flashy for his taste.

For what seemed an eternity, Young had watched others enjoy this magic moment. Now it was his turn. "I wish anyone who ever played football could feel this," he said. "It's just a great feeling."

Young had been on two other Super Bowl champions, each time as the backup for Montana, each time holding a clipboard instead of a football, wearing a baseball cap instead of a football helmet, and feeling like the loneliest guy in the building. He got the championship Super Bowl rings but always felt funny about wearing them. "I was on the team, but it was not my team," he said.

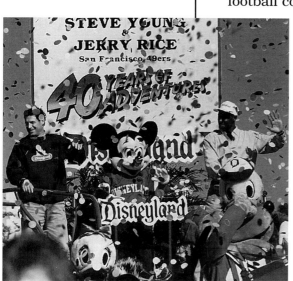

Steve Young and Jerry Rice greet the crowds during a victory parade down Main Street at Disneyland.

Those were Joe Montana's teams. He took those Niners to four world championships and was the Super Bowl MVP three times. In Montana's prime, there was no quarterback controversy. He was the man, and Young was the insurance policy. And what's more, everybody knew it.

There were times when it seemed the scenario would go on forever: Montana winning Super Bowls and Young waiting in the wings, a quarterback caddy trying to feel involved but really feeling ignored.

But nothing is forever. Injuries began to catch up with the aging Montana and the 49ers realized some changes would have to be made.

Montana forced the issue, refusing to play back-up for the man who had been his backup. Feelings were strained and eventually, San Francisco made a choice. Montana was traded to Kansas City. The 49ers were now Steve Young's team.

The transition took some time. Replacing a legend is no simple matter. There was widespread criticism, especially after Young's Niners were beaten in two straight NFC championship games by the Dallas Cowboys. The whispers were that he was a nice quarterback but that the left-hander from Brigham Young could not win the big game.

Winning two MVP titles in three years, passing for over 3,000 yards three straight seasons and setting quarterback rating records would not be enough for Young. Nothing less than a Super Bowl victory in the tradition of Joe Montana would silence the critics.

When he won it, Young clutched the Super Bowl trophy close to his chest, looking for all the world like he never intended to let go. "It feels great to win the Super Bowl, to throw six touchdowns, to play the best game you ever played," he said. "You couldn't ask for much more than that."

From across the noisy dressing room, a teammate called out to Young. "Sweet redemption, Steve!" he shouted.

Sweet redemption, indeed.

2

BRIGHAM YOUNG DAYS

If Steve Young's story was simple, he would have marched straight out of Greenwich, Connecticut, onto the campus at Brigham Young University and been a star from Day One. That is not the way it happened for Young, who always seems to take the long way around to stardom.

Jon Steven Young was born on October 11, 1961, the first child of LeGrande and Sherry Young. His father was nicknamed "Grit" when he played fullback at BYU in the 1950s, a square-jawed straight shooter whose nickname fit his style. The family moved early from Salt Lake City, Utah, to Greenwich, an affluent, leafy, well-scrubbed suburb of New York City. Grit made a good living as a corporate lawyer.

Steve Young first started playing football in Greenwich.

And baseball.

And basketball.

In his first year as a starter, Steve Young led Brigham Young University to the Holiday Bowl.

Soon there would be a brother, Mike (now a doctor in Grand Rapids, Michigan). Then a sister, Melissa. Then Tom, who followed Steve and Mike to BYU, and finally Jimmy, a high school linebacker and the only Young brother who did not become a quarterback.

The rules were simple for Grit Young's children. Take up anything you want from piano to polo. But once you do, stick to it. "He couldn't stand to watch you quit or come up short," Young said of his father.

And Steve Young never did.

He was doing push-ups at age two and dribbling a basketball at age three. He loved sports and excelled at them. And living in a neighborhood with plenty of other kids, he was always playing one thing or another, from morning until nightfall. "It was a tremendous way to grow up," Young said.

"It was pretty obvious to me that he had some gifts," Young's father said. "He was also a pretty tenacious kid, I'd say more than most kids."

By his senior year at Greenwich High School, Young was the captain of the football, baseball, and basketball teams, a leader on and off the field. He was the all-American kid, who never got caught up in teenaged pranks. He was the one the coaches could depend on in tough situations. He was the one who always seemed to score the winning touchdown, nail the winning basket, or deliver the clutch hit. He was the one parents wanted to take their daughter to the prom. He was the kid next door, almost too good to be true. And he was exactly as advertised—an uncomplicated, clean-cut kid, gifted in both athletics and academics.

With those kinds of credentials, it would seem that Young should have had his pick of colleges. But he was an option quarterback at Greenwich, throwing the ball only a half-dozen times or so each game, so the only schools that came after him were those which used that offensive scheme such as North Carolina,

Young set numerous records as a passer in college. But he already could run well, as the Baylor Bears discovered in 1983. Young dashed for the Cougars' second touchdown on this play.

Maryland, Virginia, Syracuse, and the Ivy Leagues. The option was not Young's idea. He just did what he was told. Still, the option limited his options when it came to picking a college.

Young's Mormon upbringing, and perhaps the fact that his father had played there, convinced BYU to offer Young a scholarship. It seemed entirely appropriate, since the university was named after his great-great-great-grandfather.

Nevertheless, BYU coach LaVell Edwards was not anxious to add another quarterback as he already had six, including Jim McMahon, who was widely accepted as one of the best college quarterbacks in the game. When Steve Young showed up, he was ranked at the bottom of the depth chart.

Steve Young is not a terribly complicated guy. He is pretty much a homebody, happiest when he is close to family and friends. At BYU, he was suddenly 2,000 miles away from both those groups. It was a culture shock for the kid quarterback, who never unpacked his bags that first semester and called home almost every day, hoping his folks would rescue him. He was miserable, but he was not getting much sympathy from Greenwich. "I told my dad I wanted to come home," Young said. "And he told me, 'You can quit, but you can't come home.'"

Grit Young had rules about staying with whatever you started and his eldest son was not going to break them. So Steve stuck it out, struggling through an awful freshman year that included a suggested switch to defensive back to utilize his speed. That sent chills through Young, who had never played defense and was not terribly interested in starting then. The scheme never came off because, mercifully, Ted Tollner took over as quarterback coach and decided to leave the freshman alone.

Tollner, a longtime college and pro coach, chose instead to put his fistful of quarterbacks through a competition to find a backup for starter Jim McMahon. Young, the curly-haired kid from Connecticut majoring in international relations and finance, won the understudy role and suddenly, BYU did not seem like such a terrible place after all.

Young spent most of his freshman season playing jayvee football and learning from McMahon. They were a strange pair—McMahon, a kind of loose cannon, tutoring Young, a button-down quarterback. The chemistry worked, though, and Young benefited from the relationship. McMahon, after leaving Brigham Young, led the Chicago Bears to a Super Bowl championship. A decade later, Young did the very same thing with the San Francisco 49ers.

McMahon loved to thumb his nose at authority. When NFL commissioner Pete Rozelle complained about the headband McMahon wore bearing the name of a sporting-goods company, McMahon replaced it with one that read "Rozelle" instead. At the Super Bowl he was outspoken, sometimes even offensive, exactly the opposite of Young's button-down manner.

There was no denying McMahon's talent, however. He put Brigham Young on the map by leading the nation in passing in 1980, throwing for 4571 yards and 47 touchdowns. Although his production dipped to 3555 yards and 30 touchdowns in 1981, it still was the best in the country. When he departed BYU, he left behind a legacy of success—a legacy on which Steve

Young capped his college career by leading his team to a victory in his second straight Holiday Bowl. Here he celebrates a 37–35 victory over UCLA in 1983, played in the Rose Bowl.

Young delivered.

In his sophomore year at BYU, Young got into nine games, taking over for an injured McMahon against Utah State and the University of Nevada at Las Vegas. Strangely, he had almost identical statistics in both games, completing 21 of 40 passes, gaining 307 yards against Utah State and 269 against UNLV. Perhaps his most memorable play that season came in the Holiday Bowl against Washington State University, when he was smuggled into the backfield, took a pitch from McMahon, and completed a 26-yard pass to Gordon Hudson, setting up a first-quarter touchdown.

Young finished the season with 56 completions in 111 attempts for 731 yards and five TDs as McMahon's caddy—not bad, but nothing special. Special, however, was coming up.

With McMahon gone in 1982, the quarterback job went to his backup, who until then was best known for his distant relationship to old Brigham himself. "It's interesting and fun," Young said, "but it doesn't get me anywhere."

Young had outlasted the glut of quarterbacks he found when he arrived at BYU. He had been patient, waiting his turn behind McMahon. Now it was his time and he would make the most of it. He also had some standards to live up to. Grit Young had led BYU in total offense with 423 yards one season. That would turn out to be no problem because 423 yards would be one good game or so for Grit's boy, Steve.

Young enjoyed a brilliant junior season, beginning a two-year stretch when he became the best quarterback in college football. Brigham Young was 8-4 in Young's first season as a starter and improved to 11-1 the next season. In both years, the team finished first in the Western Athletic Conference. In both years, the team advanced to the Holiday Bowl, but with vastly different results.

Even though Young had a very fine game, completing 27 of 45 passes for 341 yards, the

Cougars were blown away by Ohio State University 47–17 in the 1982 game. A year later, Young was clearly the hero in BYU's 21–17 win over the University of Missouri.

In that game, Young scored BYU's first touchdown on a 10-yard quarterback draw and then threw a 33-yard TD pass to Eddie Stinnett. Still, Missouri led 17–14 with time running out. After a goal-line stand stopped Missouri at the 6 yardline with 3:57 to play, the Cougars took over. Young led them downfield, and with one minute to play, BYU was on the Missouri 15.

Young handed off to Stinnett, who faked a sweep around the right side, then pulled up and lofted the ball back to Young. The quarterback caught the ball and scampered 15 yards for the winning score.

It was an exclamation point on a brilliant college career for Young. He had always been a running threat, and he carried 269 times for 1600 yards and 18 TDs during his college career.

In his two years as starter, Young erased a fistful of McMahon's records, not the least of them a stretch of 22 consecutive games in which he passed for over 200 yards. He threw for 3,100 yards as a junior and 3,902 yards as a senior. He completed 18 passes for touchdowns in his junior year and 33 in his senior season. Over one stretch of his junior season, he completed 22 consecutive passes—the last eight in one game against Utah State and the first 14 of his next game against the University of Wyoming. By the end of his senior season, he had broken 13 offensive records, nine of them passing. Five of the records had belonged to his old pal, Jim McMahon.

Among Young's records were most passes completed in a season (306 in 1983), most consecutive passes completed in a single game (18 versus Air Force Academy), and highest percentage of passes completed in a season (71.3 in 1983) and in a career (65.2).

Not bad for a former option quarterback.

Young's 395.1 rushing-passing yards per game in 1983 broke the record of 385.6 set by McMahon in 1980, Young's freshman year. His 3,902 passing yards in his senior season were second best in history and his 33 TD passes ranked number 5.

When it came time to award the Heisman Trophy, though, the voters chose running back Mike Rozier of Nebraska while Young finished second. That did not diminish the BYU quarterback's accomplishments, though. He was one hot property and he was about to find out just how hot.

3

DRAFT DAY DECISION

At Brigham Young University, Steve Young was a star with his feet planted firmly on the ground. He tooled around town not in some fancy sports car suited to the Heisman runner-up, but rather in a 19-year-old Oldsmobile whose best days were far behind. The beat-up car—his friends called it the Tuna Boat—suited Steve's style, though, so he nursed it along. And besides, he had time. He could buy whatever he wanted after he moved on to football's next level—the pros.

Limited to just two full seasons as BYU's starter, Young had still assembled impressive credentials and was high on the list of quarterbacks for the 1984 draft. The difference that year was that there was not just one list but two.

USFL commissioner Harry Usher shows off his league's new million-dollar quarterbacks. Steve Young (left) and Jim Kelly both went on to take their NFL teams to glory. The USFL's other bonus baby, Doug Flutie, did not have the same level of success.

The snazzy new United States Football League, complete with an attractive red, white, and blue logo, had been created to cash in on the pro football boom in America. The USFL strategy was to expand the football calendar into the spring and early summer. On the assumption that there would be more interest in the New York Giants than the New Jersey Generals, the USFL avoided a face-to-face showdown with the NFL in the traditional fall and winter, and sought instead to create a niche at a time when football was normally in recess.

Just because it chose to avoid a calendar confrontation with the established league, that did not mean the USFL was going low profile. Quite the contrary. It hired some of the most familiar names in the NFL, coaches like George Allen and Red Miller, who had taken teams to the Super Bowl. And it stocked its teams with familiar names. Heisman Trophy winner Herschel Walker signed with the Generals, running back Tim Spencer went with Allen and the Chicago Blitz, as did veteran NFL quarterback Greg Landry. Another quarterback, Brian Sipe of the Cleveland Browns, joined Walker with the Generals. Highly touted college players like quarterbacks Jim Kelly and Reggie Collier, running backs Kelvin Bryant and Craig James, wide receiver Trumaine Johnson, tackle Irv Eatman, and defensive back David Greenwood, all enrolled in the new league. A signing war was on.

There is nothing player agents like more than the establishment of a rival league. It gives their clients an option, a chance to drive up the price of a signing. History proved that in the early 1960s with the American Football League, then in the 1970s with the short-lived World Football League, and now in the 1980s with the USFL.

The USFL strategy was to buy up some identifiable NFL veterans and go after the highest profile college players. In each of its three seasons, the league signed the Heisman winner—first Walker, then Rozier, and finally, quarterback Doug Flutie. And just because Young had finished second in the Heisman, that did not mean he was any less desirable as far as the USFL was concerned.

Young's USFL rights were parceled out to the Los Angeles Express, a franchise owned by an eccentric financier, William Oldenburg. The owner of Investment Mortgage International, Oldenburg was a multimillionaire who called himself "Mr. Dynamite" and was accustomed to getting what he wanted. And in the spring of 1984, what he wanted was Steve Young.

The problem was what Young wanted. He had grown up dreaming of the NFL, idolizing quarterback Roger Staubach. He was not terribly keen about casting his lot with a rival league, despite the urging of his agent, Leigh Steinberg, a young California attorney who was developing a reputation as one of football's best player reps.

Despite Young's NFL prejudice, Steinberg insisted that he listen to the Los Angeles offer. The Express was represented in the negotiations by Don Klosterman, a longtime NFL executive and another example of the USFL stocking itself with football-savvy people. And Klosterman was determined to deliver Young. His strategy was involved. First, he signed All-American tight end Gordon Hudson, Young's teammate and

The Los Angeles Express was happy to have signed Young. The happiest person, however, may have been Leigh Steinberg (right), who negotiated the $40-million deal.

favorite receiver at BYU. The fact that Hudson had torn up his knee at the end of the 1983 season and was almost certainly not going to play in 1984 was of little relevance. It was a gesture to Young.

Then came another gesture. If Young was worried about playing behind a leaky offensive line, Klosterman took care of the problem by signing three of college football's top blockers—Mark Adickes of Baylor, Mike Reuther of Texas, and Gary Zimmerman of Oregon. And he also grabbed NFL veteran offensive lineman Jeff Hart. The message was that the Express quarterback, whoever he happened to be, would have the best protection Oldenburg's millions could buy.

Young was suitably impressed and together, Klosterman and Steinberg began hammering out an agreement, helped along when Young's NFL rights were claimed by the traditionally penurious Cincinnati Bengals. Certainly Oldenburg was not going to allow himself to be outbid by a team noted for keeping a tight lid on player salaries. The Bengals helped by making a lowball offer of $4 million for four years.

The two leagues battled hard for the quarterback. Knowing how he idolized Staubach, the

NFL had the ex-Cowboy quarterback call to woo him. The USFL responded with a call from bombastic broadcaster Howard Cosell, less seductive but certainly impressive. Perhaps more relevant was the Express coaching staff—ex-NFL quarterback John Hadl was the head coach and offensive expert Sid Gillman was the quarterback coach. This would be like learning hitting from Joe DiMaggio and Ted Williams.

As the talks headed to a conclusion, a reluctant Young joined his agent and met the cantankerous Oldenburg. The issue of guarantees came up and Oldenburg wadded up a handful of large bills and tossed them contemptuously at the feet of the quarterback and his agent. "Here's all the guarantees you'll need," he snarled. This was not exactly out of the primer of how to win friends and influence people, something that was of little concern to Oldenburg.

In the course of a nightlong meeting, the owner started jabbing Young in the chest to make a point. The quarterback responded in anger, saying pointedly, "If you touch me one more time, I'll deck you."

Clearly, things were not going well. It seemed the deal was doomed. But Steinberg and Klosterman were determined not to let it fall apart. And with Oldenburg's open checkbook providing the ammunition, the two sides reached an agreement on March 5, 1984. Young would receive a $2.5 million signing bonus followed by salaries that escalated from $300,000 to $600,000 followed by a $37.2 million annuity that would trigger in 1997. Total value of the deal: $40 million, at the time the richest contract in professional sports. It was a far cry from

J. William Oldenburg's contract called for Young to receive more money than any other athlete ever. The Express, though, folded long before it had paid Young a significant portion of that contract.

Klosterman's original offer: $6 million for four years or one-third more than the Bengals were offering. This was not one-third more. This was 10 times more.

Klosterman was ecstatic. "I can't remember another signing that would match this," he said. "I guess you'd have to go back to Joe Namath's signing with the New York Jets. It's a tremendous step forward for the league."

If Klosterman was thrilled, Young was not. He had signed, but not with a great deal of enthusiasm. He walked around with the bonus check in his pocket for a week without cashing it, then turned the thing over to Steinberg. He was disgusted with himself for succumbing, so disgusted, in fact, that he thought about not reporting to the Express.

"The money just overwhelmed him," said Grit Young, Steve's father. "The money became his nemesis and he continued to live as if he did not have it. He told me before he had to report to camp, 'I don't want to go.' I ended up having to go out to Provo to talk to him. I told him, 'You made a contract; you live up to the contract.'"

Young had heard this speech before. It was shades of his freshman year at BYU all over again—the reluctant quarterback regretting an important career decision and his father insisting that he stick to his commitment.

As always, Young followed his father's advice. It was not something he did cheerfully or enthusiastically, though. "I felt my life was never going to be the same," he said. "I felt in some way, my life was going down the tubes. You're in crisis and the whole world gets to watch."

He had not seen anything yet. The crisis was still ahead.

4

ADVENTURES WITH THE EXPRESS

Two days after the Los Angeles Express lost its second straight game in its second season, Steve Young signed his fancy new contract and joined the team. This was not destined to be the perfect marriage, regardless of how much Young was making, and he was making plenty.

The base salary was $300,000 but there were all sorts of attachments, the most impressive being the huge annuity due to kick in beginning in 1997. By 1997, though, Bill Oldenburg, the LA Express, and, in fact, the whole USFL would be long gone. That came as no surprise to Young. A month after he had enrolled in the venture, he had predicted its demise.

"I really feel like the NFL is going to quietly take on about four or five teams—very exciting ball clubs—and then watch the great of the league go by the wayside," Young said. "I don't

Young had a hard time finding receivers downfield, or blockers fending off the rush, as he struggled at quarterback with the poor Express.

think two leagues can exist. I don't think there's ever been a situation where two leagues can compete for a long period of time. So I think that is going to happen sooner than people think."

USFL executives were not amused by Young's pop off. Here was one of the league's marquee players spouting off all this negative stuff. Not good. Not good at all. Young knew his history though. The World Football League had challenged the NFL and lost. So had the American Football League and before that, the All-America Conference. Teams from both those ventures had been absorbed. Young figured the same thing would happen again.

Within a day after his remarks were reported, Young backed off. "I got involved in league politics and I shouldn't have," he said. "I learned my lesson, and I'll bear the brunt for it. I hope people don't make a big deal of it.... I'm not perfect. I feel horrible. I'm still young and I haven't learned yet what you can say and what you can't. I'll be careful from now on."

That was just the beginning of what Young now refers to as "a very bizarre and crazy time." That seems to be an understatement. Life with the Express was anything but predictable and although it may have delayed Young's development somewhat, he is not bitter over the experience. "I look back on those days with fondness," he said. "A lot of the teammates that I had and the people that I knew are friends to this day. I know my career has taken some strange turns. If what happened throughout that time got me to where I am today—Super Bowl MVP—then let me go back there and start over again."

There were great moments for the young passer from BYU. In one game against Chicago, he became the first player in pro football history to rush for 100 yards and pass for 300 in the same game. He was a multitalented quarterback, equipped with great tools and a lust to learn the game. For that, at least, he had come to the right place.

Part of the inducement for Young to sign with the LA Express was the fact that the team's coaching staff included Sid Gillman, considered one of football's greatest offensive minds. "I feel like I did a substantial part of my growing up as a quarterback in the USFL because Sid Gillman was my quarterback coach," he said. "I look at what I learned from him as being a kind of foundation for me. Sid was probably the first one who took me aside and said, 'You're a little wild. We need to corral you.' I have heeded that ever since."

Gillman was a crusty old coach, accustomed to explaining offense without many frills. Young was a 21-year-old Mormon. They were the odd couple of the Express, spending hours together, just talking football—history, theories. It was like an offensive laboratory for the young quarterback.

Even though he was making big money, Young's LA Express days were sort of like an extension of college. He lived with six teammates in a Redondo Beach apartment that could have just as well been a BYU dormitory. He nursed the old Oldsmobile along, happy, he once said, if he had $20 in his pocket and a tank full of gas in the car. After the Super Bowl, someone wondered about the fate of the old Olds. "I gave it to my brother," he said. "He wouldn't change the oil and it died. No respect."

The money never changed Young, certainly

not with respect to his relationship with his family, especially his brothers. When the $40 million quarterback came home to Connecticut after his first pro season, his brother Mike was sick with a virus and could not handle his paper route. No problem. Steve pinch-hit. It was an opportunity to help his brother and, at the same time, return a little sanity to his own life, a condition largely absent around the Express.

With Oldenburg and his trigger temper operating the team, things did not always go smoothly. One day, the owner became angry over low ticket sales for the season opener and summoned his staff to a summit meeting at a Los Angeles restaurant. If necessary, he said, he would send his people out on street corners to sell tickets. He went off on a tirade that would have made George Steinbrenner proud, capping the show by hurling a plate of food at Express coach John Hadl. It missed.

Hadl, an ex-quarterback, retrieved the plate and hurled it back at Oldenburg. The coach's All-Pro days were behind him, though. He missed, too.

It was about this time that Oldenburg's financial empire began unraveling. Banking authorities in Utah were looking into a savings and loan institution he had purchased. His reported $100 million portfolio was beginning to appear to be worth considerably less than that. USFL officials began noticing and feeling a tad squeamish about one of the league's glamour franchises. So, too, did people who were doing business with the team.

Bills began not getting paid—hardly the way to do business. Sometimes, the explanation was the traditional one of "the check is in the mail." It rarely turned out to be, though.

Plumbers were not paid. Painters were not paid. Hotels were not paid. Truck companies were not paid. The list goes on and on. And in the middle of it was the quarterback with the golden arm, who had emerged as the leader of the team. In 1985, the final season for the Express, there was one financial crisis after another. The tone was

Sid Gillman worriedly looks over the field as does quarterback Tom Ramsey (center) and the newly signed Steve Young.

set in training camp when the club was evicted from its hotel headquarters for failing to pay the bill. Players billeted in apartments as if they were in college dorms.

The final home game of the season was to be played at a junior college—that is how far the Express had fallen. A bus carrying the players— all in uniform—pulled to the side of the road and the driver demanded his money. Failure to pay would leave the players stranded. There was some reluctance but eventually they passed the

Young has his arms in the air as if he is signaling to give up. Indeed, Vito McKeever (#36) is about to tackle Young for a loss as the Oakland Invaders crush the Express 27–6.

hat and collected the fee, with the bulk of the money coming from the guy who could best afford it—the $40-million quarterback.

By then, the Express roster had thinned out. Players who were injured were not replaced. At the end of the season, Hadl was down to one healthy running back, Mel Gray, and when Gray went down in the third quarter of the final game, Young went to the coach and volunteered to play tailback. He was a pretty good running quarterback so why not?

"He was going to put a lineman in," Young said. "I went to him and said I'd go in for a few plays." The quarterback made some blocks and escaped in one piece. The running back crisis, however, was typical of how desperate the Express's situation had become.

Junior college fields, staff cuts all over the place, no training headquarters, a trail of unpaid bills—the Express had become the poster child for financial disaster, losing $20 million in three seasons and leaving about $1 million in unpaid bills to a variety of debtors. In six months under Oldenburg's stewardship, the team had spent $12 million on players.

When it became apparent that Oldenburg's house of cards was beginning to shudder, the league stepped in, determined to save the LA Express franchise. Costs were cut everywhere, from the firing of Klosterman, Hadl, and the reputable football people to the dismissal of the cheerleaders. The number one cost to be cut was the $40 million quarterback.

This would not be a problem with Young, who had not been thrilled from day one with the USFL adventure and wanted out unless he could be assured of some stability. That commodity had been missing for a long time, though.

"It was kind of unbelievable," Young said of the 3-15 season. "I had never been associated with a losing team in my whole life. Not in Greenwich, not at Brigham Young. But this year was one thing going wrong after another. It was a struggle for everyone involved. Everyone in the world would like to have a little stability.

"Up to now, I've played a lot of football through adversity. Even though it was horrible and you don't want to have it happen to you, I've learned from it. I'm trying to think of the positives."

In February, after the league takeover, Young's agent, Leigh Steinberg, contacted commissioner Harry Usher claiming his client's no trade contract had been violated when the league took control of the franchise. "It is our very strong and considered conclusion that Steve's contract was breached when it was assigned to the league," Steinberg said. "There is a clause in Steve's contract which was bargained and fought over—it was specifically inserted—that says, unlike other contracts, Steve's contract could not be assigned to other clubs or to the league itself."

Usher dismissed the claim. As much as he wanted to unload the obligation of Young's contract, he also knew the Express would be a lot less desirable to prospective buyers without the quarterback.

Eventually, though, the commissioner realized hanging onto Young would mean a messy court fight and he chose to retreat, allowing the quarterback to buy his way out of the last two years of his contract for $1.2 million. The price was "a king's ransom," Steinberg said. In a prepared statement, Usher said, "We felt that in the best interests of both Steve Young and the USFL that he should be released from his contract. Because of the Express's disappointing year, he has asked to be released. We have agreed to negotiate a buyout. He's an exciting player who was a credit to our league and we wish him well in his pro football future."

He did not mention the price of the release.

For Young, the Express adventure ended mercifully. He had passed for 2,361 yards in his first year, throwing 10 TDs, and 9 interceptions. Battling injuries and off-the-field mayhem, he threw for 1,741 yards, 6 touchdowns and 13 interceptions in his second season. He earned $5 million in two seasons with the Express and the buyout fee matched the signing bonus he received from the NFL Tampa Bay Buccaneers, who had picked him in a special NFL supplemental draft of USFL players.

The USFL experiment had become a fiasco, ominously reminiscent of the final days of the World Football League. Young, it seemed, had been right from the beginning. This league was not going to be around very long after all.

The USFL's last gasp was a $1.32 billion antitrust lawsuit filed against the NFL. The jury awarded one dollar in damages. As in all antitrust cases, the award was trebled—to three dollars. The USFL was history and so was its most famous contract.

"I'll always be remembered for the $40 million thing and I've always disliked that," Young said. "I'm not on a crusade to prove that money is not important, but I live the way I live."

Which is to say jeans and T-shirts, jackets and ties only when absolutely necessary, and a beat-up 1965 Olds with its oil changed periodically. So Young packed up and moved from one coast to the other, from L.A. to Tampa Bay, for what would turn out to be another less-than-satisfying pit stop on the way to success.

5

ESCAPE TO TAMPA

In the war between the USFL and NFL, the players were the pawns, claimed as trophies by one against the other. Some teams chose to sign veteran marquee names for instant recognition. Don Klosterman's approach with the LA Express was to raid the college ranks and sign as many prospects as he could. Steve Young was the crown jewel in that collection.

While the NFL's public policy was to ignore the infidels with that snappy red, white, and blue logo, privately the established league recognized that there was some legitimate talent operating on the other side of the pro football street. Just in case the USFL spent itself into oblivion, the NFL decided to conduct what it called a supplemental draft to divide up the other league's talent. The first pick in that draft belonged to Tampa Bay and the Bucs claimed the rights to Young.

Steve Young was relieved to move to the Tampa Bay Buccaneers. The team had enough money to pay its bills, but its success on the field was no greater than that of the Los Angeles Express.

When Young and the USFL agreed to go their separate ways, it took two months to work out a deal with Tampa Bay. This was a franchise that never rushed into anything. The Bucs lost their first 26 regular season games before they got around to winning one. That was during John McKay's regime. Leeman Bennett was the coach when the team signed Young, and he was enthusiastic about the quarterback.

"Mind, feet, and arm," Bennett said, "we think he's got a tremendous future."

Thirty-one-year-old Steve DeBerg was Tampa Bay's quarterback in 1985 and Young was supposed to be in training to take over the job down the road. Learn at the old guy's knee for a while and then replace him later. It was a pattern that would haunt Young for years to come. At the time, though, he would say all the right things and sound properly contrite. It was the least he could do after being rescued from the merry-go-round in L.A.

"I'm not walking into Tampa expecting anything but what I earn," Young said. "I don't want to get in any kind of situation where people expect you to play because you showed up. No one walks in and just takes over."

"We expect him to come in and learn our system and be a backup quarterback to Steve DeBerg for a while," Bennett said. "How soon he'll play depends on how soon he'll be ready to play. But obviously, we feel he's got a bright future in this league or else we wouldn't have made the investment."

The investment was a six-year $5-million deal, a far cry from the USFL bank-buster.

Young did not make his first start for the Bucs until their 11th game of the 1985 season. The Bucs had lost 10 of those games.

These, though, were real dollars, not Monopoly money, and Young was more than pleased with the contract. Not much else went right for him with the Bucs, though.

Bennett was a conservative coach who preferred a traditional pocket passer. Young was a scrambler who loved to run with the ball. It was not the very best of matches. In addition, Young did not sign with the Bucs until the middle of September, missing training camp. There are better ways for a quarterback to start out with a new franchise. There are also better franchises for a quarterback than those woebegone Bucs.

True to his word, Bennett did not rush Young into the fray. The left-hander from BYU was not handed the football until 11 games into the season. Tampa Bay had lost 10 of them. This was the LA Express all over again. The only difference was the Bucs paid their bills.

Young became the 13th starting quarterback in the Bucs' 10-year history. He was the fifth in four years. And this was a guy looking for football stability. His performance was shaky at best. He went 1-4 with three touchdowns and eight interceptions. It was not pretty.

Some people began questioning his arm strength and Young bristled at the criticism.

"I've heard the talk," he said, "but it doesn't bother me because I know from watching other people that as far as arm strength goes, there are people who have been very successful with less—Joe Montana to name one."

Interesting that he would choose that name.

"It always has to be something with young quarterbacks," Young continued. "John Elway was 'confused' before he arrived. Warren Moon was 'good in Canada but not in the NFL,' before he arrived. Until I'm in the starting lineup and winning games, until I prove myself, it's always going to be something. As far as my confidence, the talk doesn't bother me one bit."

Bennett noted that in his five-game trial in 1985, Young had lacked poise and played somewhat helter-skelter football. That, of course, was easy to do behind the Bucs' leaky offensive line.

With Young on the sidelines for most of his first year in Tampa Bay, the Bucs were 2-14. Allowed to play the next season, the record was again 2-14. This was a team on a treadmill, headed nowhere and getting there in a hurry. Young threw for 2,282 yards with eight touchdowns and 13 interceptions. In one game against the Green Bay Packers, he was smashed so hard into the snow that the ice had to be immediately cleared from his helmet so he could breathe. As the season drew to a close with a final loss, again to Green Bay, he said, "I played my heart out this year. I've always been battling. There's been progress made this year but going out like this, there's a distaste."

As always with a bleeding football team, the buzzards circled first around the coach and then around the quarterback. Bennett was fired, replaced by Ray Perkins, who also had a somewhat buttoned-down view of how his quarterback ought to play. The 2-14 record had clinched another number one draft choice for Tampa Bay. The year before, they had used their number one pick to draft Auburn University running back Bo Jackson, who took one look at the Bucs and told them, "Thanks, but no thanks," choosing instead to play baseball. This time the obvious number one choice was University of Miami quarterback Vinny Testaverde. With Perkins's blessing, the Bucs committed themselves to him.

This made Young and his contract expendable, and four days before the 1987 NFL draft, the Bucs found a taker. Coach Bill Walsh in San Francisco was shopping for a backup to Joe Montana and he liked what he saw in Young. Walsh had always had an eye for quarterbacks. He drafted Montana with a third-round pick. The price for Young seemed reasonable—two draft choices, one in the second round, the other in the fourth, and $1 million to compensate the Bucs for the signing bonus they had laid out two years earlier.

Perkins was asked if he had surrendered Young a little cheaply. "Well," the coach noted, "nobody was knocking down the door."

Walsh made it clear that trading for Young did not constitute any threat to his starter, Montana. "We fully expect Joe to continue as the leader and mainstay of our team," he said. "But we have a great deal of regard for Young's athletic ability, quick release and fine instincts. He is probably the fastest running quarterback in the league and his play is similar to that of Montana."

The trade also reunited Young with Mike Holmgren, then the 49ers quarterbacks coach, who had been at BYU. That made it a comfortable fit for all concerned.

Left unsaid was the fact that Young seemed a perfect insurance policy. At 25, he was five years younger than Montana. Teams get a little squeamish when their quarterbacks hit 30. What Walsh—and Young—did not know was that Montana would go on for years to come.

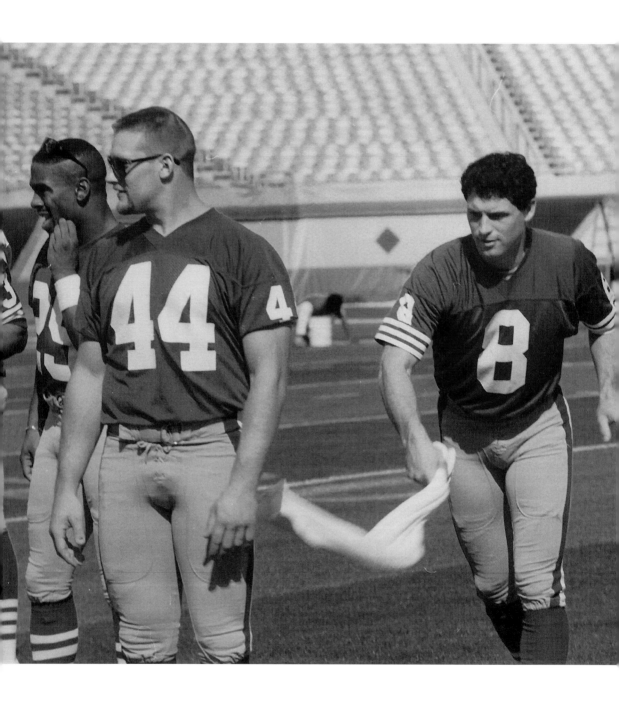

6

CALIFORNIA, HERE I COME

W hen he traded for Young, Walsh did not make it sound like any big deal. It was to him, though. The 49ers coach had scouted Young at BYU, where the quarterback worked out in the off-season while attending law school, and he liked what he saw. He had heard nothing but good things from respected NFL people about the left-hander from BYU, things that made him believe Young had been victimized by his surroundings, not his abilities.

Still, San Francisco had Joe Montana, perhaps the best quarterback of his time, who had taken the team to two Super Bowl championships. As much as he was intrigued by Young's talent, Walsh was not about to disturb the chemistry of the 49ers by making a sudden change. He did like the idea, though, of having a talented relief pitcher available, just in case. The year before, Montana had missed two months

Steve Young could afford to be loose before the 1989 Super Bowl. Tom Rathman (#44) was the starting fullback. Young was the backup quarterback.

because of back problems. Walsh wanted protection if something like that happened again.

Somehow, Steve Young's arrival revitalized Montana. It was as if he had turned into Ponce de Leon and located pro football's Fountain of Youth. Each year there would be talk of an open competition for quarterback and speculation about how much longer Montana could go on. And each year, he played like a kid. He took the Niners to two more Super Bowls, all the time with Young on the sidelines, cooling his heels, wondering where football had gone wrong for him.

Every so often, Walsh would plug Young in, just to get him some game action. Montana always seemed annoyed with that strategy—he always suspected Young was lobbying for more playing time. There was a basic personality clash between the two quarterbacks.

Montana was fun loving and viewed Young as a goody-two-shoes. Quarterback meetings were not always the most pleasant places, especially with Mike Holmgren, Young's old BYU coach, handling the 49ers offense. Montana figured Holmgren was in Young's corner. Tension clearly was in the air.

Still, though, the 49ers won, and by and large Young waited. He would start just 10 games in four seasons. His playing time came mostly when Montana was banged up. The rest of the time, he would stand on the sidelines, wearing a baseball cap and carrying a clipboard. It was not the most exciting job in the world, although the salary was good.

Young would get two Super Bowl rings—jewelry he never wore, partly because he is not a jewelry guy and partly because he felt he had not earned them. "Those were Joe's teams," he would say later. "When you're not playing, you're not part of the team. You're not contributing.

"It's frustrating to sit and wait. That was a tough time. Sometimes tough means good. I'm now grateful for the tough times. I appreciate it."

Montana owned the town in those days and Young knew it. "If you lived in the Bay Area you had to be caught up in those days—the four Super Bowls."

In 1991, Young almost had his own Super Bowl. Montana was kayoed by the New York Giants late in the NFC championship game and Young replaced him, throwing a 25-yard completion on his only pass attempt. The Giants rallied and won the game and a ticket to the Super Bowl. Had the 49ers won, with Montana out Young would have started the Super Bowl. Instead, he went home to contemplate his future. He was almost 30—the witching age for quarterbacks—and he was still waiting in the wings, a silent partner, frustrated and disillusioned. His contract was up and agent Leigh Steinberg was just as fed up as his client and suggested pushing for a trade.

Certainly, Young thought about it. "I think, primarily, I just wanted to get on the field," he said. "I just couldn't take it anymore. I think it was obvious to everyone who I talked to that I wanted to do it in San Francisco if I could. But

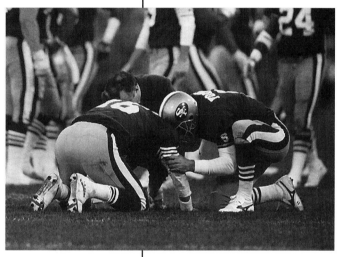

After Leonard Marshall popped Joe Montana in the 1991 NFC championship game, Young went to help out his teammate. Steve played the rest of the game, which the Giants won, 15–13.

Ah, what a good team can do for you! In this 1993 game against the Lions, Steve Young threw for 4 touchdowns and 352 yards—and his coach took him out during the third quarter!

who knew? It was really hard to predict how everything was going to pan out."

Walsh had left the club after the third Super Bowl in 1989, replaced by George Seifert, who coached the 49ers to number four the next year with Montana still at the quarterback helm. Seifert knew Young was getting antsy and tried to comfort him by guaranteeing him three or four starts the next season. Young reenlisted and when Montana got wind of the deal, he went ballistic. The relationship between the quarterbacks, already tense, soured even more.

In 1991, after the NFC championship game knockout by the Giants, Montana needed elbow surgery and finally, Walsh's insurance policy would pay off. Seifert's guaranteed three or four starts became a full-time assignment for Young and he responded brilliantly. He set two team records, completing 90 percent of his attempts (18-for-20) against Detroit and connecting with John Taylor for a 97-yard TD against the Atlanta Falcons. He was the NFC offensive player of the month for October.

Young would start 10 games, his season interrupted by a knee injury, and win the NFL passing title with a rating of 101.8. But it was not without controversy. The 49ers were just 5-5 in his starts and when backup Steve Bono won five straight games while Young was out, the whole Bay Area became Bono boosters.

The team had missed the playoffs for the first time in nine years and despite impressive individual numbers—2,517 yards and 17 touchdowns—Young was the scapegoat. The fans wanted Montana back and if they could not have him, they wanted Bono. But Seifert, the only one who really mattered, wanted Young. So with Montana still recovering in 1992, Young was the starter again. And this time, he left no questions about whether he deserved the job.

Young was merely brilliant in 1992. He led the league in all four categories that make up passing rankings—completion percentage (66.7); average yards per attempt (8.62); TD passes (25); and interception percentage (1.7). It added up to his second straight passing title and a ranking of 107.0, the first time any quarterback had back-to-back seasons of ratings over 100. He threw for 3,465 yards, leading the 49ers to a 14-2 season, and he was an easy choice as the league's MVP.

And yet, in this best of all possible seasons, there was still the shadow of Montana. He had recuperated and in the last week of the season, he was activated. Given the ball for the second half of the season finale against Detroit, Montana responded brilliantly, completing 15 of 21 passes for 126 yards and two touchdowns. Now it was Young's turn to be livid. Here he was the league's MVP and two-time passing champion and the 49ers could not wait to give the ball back to Montana.

In the playoffs, Young played poorly. There were three fumbles and an interception in the first game against the Washington Redskins and two more interceptions in the NFC championship game loss against the Dallas Cowboys. Once again, Young was on the hot seat. His contract was up, Montana was healed and a season of great accomplishments had ended on a sour note. Clearly, there were some decisions to be made.

The first one concerned Montana. After two years of virtually no action, he was ready to reclaim his job and that meant as a starter, not a backup. What's more, the 49ers, troubled by the playoff failure, seemed for a time inclined to let him have it. At least briefly, they considered trading Young and drafting a quarterback to serve as Montana's new caddy.

When the 49ers finally made their choice, though, it was Montana, not Young, who was sent packing. Kansas City was happy to turn its offense over to the man who owned four Super Bowl rings. The quarterback controversy in San Francisco was over, at last.

Having committed themselves to Young, the 49ers signed him to the richest contract in NFL history, a five-year deal worth $26.75 million. "Steve has been a solid member of this team," said club president Carmen Policy. "He's always been there when we needed him. Even if he did not agree with what was happening on the field or off the field, he never turned his back on the organization. And I think it was time the organization recognized that."

As usual, Young was matter-of-fact about the money. "Frankly, he was never concerned about the money," agent Steinberg said. "At no time during the negotiations did he as so much ask about it. All he's ever wanted is what he has now—and that's to start."

Turned loose, with no need to look over his shoulder, Young produced another brilliant season in 1993. Despite a broken thumb in pre-season and a number of concussions, he led the league in passing for the third straight year, this time with a rating of 101.5—the first time any passer had three straight 100-plus ratings. He threw for 4,023 yards, a club record and the first 49ers quarterback to go over 4,000 yards in a season. There was a string of 183 consecutive passes without an interception, another club record.

The team finished 10-6 and again reached the NFC championship game. Once again, Dallas was waiting, and again, Young came up empty at the end, beaten decisively by the Cowboys, 38–21. Once again, the whispers started around the Bay Area. Steve Young could do a lot of things for you. He could run and throw and lead the world in passing. But the one thing he could not do, the one thing Joe Montana always did, was win the big game.

The next season, Young would end those whispers permanently.

7

THAT CHAMPIONSHIP SEASON

Before the start of the 1994 season, the 49ers' front office did some brilliant salary cap maneuvering and brought in cornerback Deion Sanders, center Bart Oates, linebackers Gary Plummer and Ken Norton, Jr., and defensive linemen Richard Dent and Rickey Jackson. Steve Young, owner of three straight passing titles led the all-star lineup.

The 49ers opened at home against the Los Angeles Raiders and on their first two possessions, Young threw TD passes. The first one came on San Francisco's fourth play from scrimmage, when Young connected with Jerry Rice on what became a 69-yard TD. It was the first of three TDs Rice scored that day, pushing his career total to 127 and breaking Jim Brown's NFL mark of 126. Young was 19 of 32 for 308 yards and four TDs in a 44–14 romp.

San Francisco showed it was a team of destiny in the very first game of the 1994 season. Here Young escapes Raiders' defensive end Scott Davis. Steve threw for 308 yards and 4 touchdowns in the 49ers' 44–14 victory.

Next came a game at Kansas City, an emotional meeting of 49ers quarterbacks past and present. Nostalgia won. Joe Montana, playing inspired football, led the Chiefs to a 24–17 victory. Young was gracious about the outcome. "In a lot of ways, I guess it shows the master had some more to teach the student," he said.

A week later, the 49ers bounced back, beating the Los Angeles Rams 34–19. Young completed 31 of 39 passes for 355 yards, threw for two TDs, ran for two more, and threw a huge block, clearing the way for a TD on a reverse by Rice. The Niners followed that with a 24–13 win over New Orleans.

The Eagles scored two touchdowns in the first quarter of the next game and two more in the second. In the third quarter of the 40–8 embarrassment, Young was yanked from the game, completing just 11 passes and throwing two interceptions. On the sidelines, he got into a shouting match with coach George Seifert.

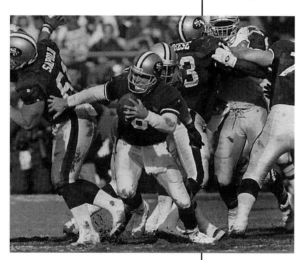

Young's scrambling helped the 49ers jump out to a 21–0 lead in the first quarter of the NFC championship game against the two-time world champion Dallas Cowboys.

Later Seifert and Young talked it out. "He apologized," the quarterback said. "That was pretty neat."

A week later, the crisis deepened. Only 3-2 after five games, the 49ers were down 14–0 at Detroit. San Francisco recovered to win 27–21, though, scoring the next four touchdowns, the final one on a pass by Young.

Now the 49ers began to roll. Young completed 15 of 16 passes, four of them for touchdowns, the next week in a 42–3 blowout of Atlanta. Then it was 20 of 26 for 255 yards as the 49ers punished Tampa Bay 41–16. Young's only TD pitch the next week was a 69-yard connection with tight end Brent Jones, the longest reception of Jones's career, as San Francisco defeated Washington, 37–22.

At 7–2, the 49ers were ready for the biggest game of the regular season with Dallas coming into Candlestick Park. Young was equal to the task. He ran for one TD, then passed for two others in a 21–14 victory. It was as important to the 49ers' psyches as it was in the standings. At last, they had conquered the Cowboys.

Young completed 30 of 44 passes for 325 yards and four touchdowns against the Los Angeles Rams and the 49ers needed them all in a 31–27 victory. There were four more TD passes the next week in a 35–14 romp over New Orleans. Then the 49ers destroyed Atlanta 50–14 with Young passing for three TDs and running for two others. San Francisco next defeated San Diego 38–15, a 23-point margin of victory that would be duplicated in the Super Bowl. Young was 25 of 32 for 304 yards and two TDs and completed his last 13 in a row that day. Denver was the 49ers' 10th victim in a row. Young was 20 of 29 for 350 yards and three TDs in the 42–19 win.

With the division title and home field advantage safely secured, Seifert rested some of his regulars in the season's final game, a 21–14 loss at Minnesota. Before he left the game, Young threw 13 passes and completed 12 of them.

Young finished the season completing 324 of 461 passes for 3,969 yards and 35 touchdowns. He had a completion percentage of 70.3 and a record-busting quarterback rating of 112.8—his fourth straight passing title and fourth straight year with a rating of over 100.

It was no contest for MVP and Young was

After playing for many years on bad teams and after backing up a great quarterback for several years, finally Steve Young got to show that he was a terrific player too.

suitably humble about the award.

"When we're talking about MVP in the league, that's supposed to be once in a lifetime," he said. "Twice in a lifetime, whew. They're both very special to me."

Against the Bears in the divisional playoff, San Francisco enjoyed a 44–15 cakewalk, made memorable by Young's six-yard TD run just before halftime.

Finally, came the NFC championship game and for the third straight year, it was San Francisco against Dallas in the season's most widely anticipated game. The Cowboys had lorded it over the 49ers on their way to two straight Super Bowl titles. This time, though, the tables were turned.

The game was barely a minute old when Eric Davis returned an interception 44 yards for a TD. Then Davis forced a fumble that Young converted into a 29-yard TD pass to Ricky Watters. Another fumble led to another 49er TD, and 7½ minutes into the game San Francisco led 21–0. "We knew they were not going to quit," Young said, "because I know if we were down 21–0, we wouldn't have."

Predictably, the Cowboys came back. But the three-touchdown hole was too deep. Young ran three yards for the wrap-up TD in a 38-28 victory that sent the 49ers to the Super Bowl and their quarterback to his greatest triumph.

As the championship game ended, Young took a victory lap around Candlestick Park, sharing the joy he felt with the fans.

Joe Montana was a memory now, replaced by a curly-haired kid from Connecticut, the great-great-great grandson of Brigham Young, who has turned out to be pretty great himself.

STEVE YOUNG:
A CHRONOLOGY

1961   Born Jon Steven Young, October 11, 1961, at Salt Lake City, Utah.

1979   Graduates from Greenwich, Connecticut, High School and enrolls
        in Brigham Young University, named for his great-great-great-
        grandfather.

1983   Heisman Trophy runner-up and consensus All-American. In his final
        year at BYU posts a completion percentage of 71.3 on 306-for-429,
        3,902 yards, and 33 touchdowns, at the time the highest single season
        percentage in NCAA history.

1983   Drafted by Cincinnati Bengals in NFL and Los Angeles Express in
        L.A. Signs richest-ever pro contract at the time, agreeing to a $40-
        million deal with the Express.

1985   Buys out his USFL contract and signs with Tampa Bay Bucs.

1987   Traded by Tampa Bay to San Francisco the day before the draft for a
        pair of picks, one in the second round, the other in the fourth.

1991   NFL leader in passing efficiency with 101.8 quarterback rating.

1992   NFL MVP. Wins second straight passing title with quarterback rating
        of 107.

1993   Leads league in touchdown passes (29) and quarterback rating (101.5),
        a record third straight passing title.

1994   NFL regular season and Super Bowl MVP. Sets quarterback rating
        record of 112.8, extending his own record to four straight
        passing titles.

STATISTICS

STEVE YOUNG
NFL STATISTICS

YEAR	Passing						Rushing			
	ATT	COM	YDS	PCT	INT	TD	ATT	YDS	AVG	TD
1985	138	72	935	.522	8	3	40	233	5.8	1
1986	363	195	2282	.537	13	8	74	425	3.5	5
1987	69	37	570	.536	0	10	26	190	7.3	1
1988	101	54	680	.535	3	3	27	184	6.8	1
1989	92	64	1001	.696	3	8	38	126	3.3	2
1990	62	38	427	.613	0	2	15	159	10.6	0
1991	279	180	2517	.645	8	17	65	415	6.3	4
1992	402	268	3465	.667	7	25	75	537	7.1	4
1993	462	314	4023	.680	16	29	69	407	5.9	2
1994	461	324	3969	.703	10	35	58	293	5.1	7
Totals	2429	1546	19,869	.636	68	140	489	2969	6.1	27

ATT	attempts
COM	completed
YDS	yards
PCT	percent
INT	interceptions
TD	touchdowns
AVG	average

SUGGESTIONS FOR FURTHER READING

Arneson, D.J. *Football's Awesome Quarterbacks.* Racine, WI: Western Publishing Company, 1991.

Montana, Joe, and Bob Raissman. *Audibles: My Life in Football.* New York: Avon Books, 1986.

Tuckman, Michael W., and Jeff Schultz. *The San Francisco 49ers: Team of the Decade.* Rocklin, CA: Prima Publishing, 1990.

ABOUT THE AUTHOR

Hal Bock has written about sports for the Associated Press since 1963, covering every major event including the Olympic Games, the World Series, the Kentucky Derby, the Indy 500, Wimbledon, the U.S. Open, and the Final Four, plus championship fights and college football bowls. He has covered 23 Super Bowls, including all five won by the 49ers.

Bock, a native of New York City and a journalism graduate of New York University, has won five Associated Press Sports Editors awards. He lives on Long Island with his wife, a psychologist.

INDEX

PICTURE CREDITS

AP/Wide World Photos: 2, 8, 12, 14, 17, 20, 24, 28, 30, 37, 38, 48, 51, 52, 56, 58, 60; UPI/Bettmann: 32;
Courtesy Tampa Bay Buccaneers: 42, 44.